I See Kitty

Yasmine Surovec

ROARING BROOK PRESS

New York

Chloe loves kitties.

She loves their quiet purrs

Purr
Purr

and their soft, cuddly fur.

She loves their
fluffy bellies,

their pink paws,

and their dainty little noses.

Sniff

Sniff

Now Chloe sees
Kitty everywhere
she goes.

At night, Chloe climbs
into her bed . . .

and sees Kitty
in her dreams.

When she wakes up, Chloe hears something outside her bedroom door.

To Victor, my family,
and to all budding cat ladies and gents

Copyright © 2013 by Yasmine Surovec
Published by Roaring Brook Press
Roaring Brook Press is a division of Holtzbrinck Publishing Holdings Limited Partnership
175 Fifth Avenue, New York, New York 10010
mackids.com

Library of Congress Cataloging-in-Publication Data
Surovec, Yasmine, author, illustrator.
I see Kitty / Yasmine Surovec.
pages   cm
Summary: Chloe wants a kitten so badly that she imagines she sees cats
all around her town, until her mother brings her a kitten of her own.
ISBN 978-1-59643-862-0 (hardcover)
[1. Cats—Fiction.   2. Animals—Infancy—Fiction.]   I. Title.

PZ7.S965626Iah 2013
[E]—dc23
                                                          2012050306

Roaring Brook Press books may be purchased for business or promotional use.
For information on bulk purchases please contact Macmillan Corporate and Premium Sales Department
at (800) 221-7945 x5442 or by email at specialmarkets@macmillan.com.

First edition 2013

Book design by Roberta Pressel
Printed in China by South China Printing Co. Ltd., Dongguan City, Guangdong Province

1   3   5   7   9   10   8   6   4   2